FOREWORD

I love this book! *Sorry Day* is a beautiful concept and wonderfully illustrated. The story of two young girls from the same family, but from different times, is cleverly entwined. From the dark there can be a glimmer of light. Our history is important and the more we learn together the more we can grow.

With information about the Stolen Generations and National Sorry Day at the end of the story, this book helps us to educate all Australians about the recent history of our people and our country and to understand why our nation pauses to say sorry.

Lee Joachim

Chief Executive Officer of Rumbalara Aboriginal Co-operative; Director of Research and Development, Yorta Yorta Nation Aboriginal Corporation

Sorry Day

Coral Vass and Dub Leffler

NLA PUBLISHING

There was a hum of excitement.

Flags flickered in the breeze as Maggie's heart danced with delight.

'This is a very special day!' her mother said.

Long ago and not so long ago, the women sat around the hissing fire. The smell of breakfast flooded the camp as flies circled above. Running in the morning sun, the children kicked up dust.

Maggie twirled around her mother's legs, in and out, playing hide-and-seek.

The crowd hushed. Every eye was locked on the giant screen as a man began to speak.

Maggie's mother leaned down, 'Shhh! Listen.'

Racing each other to the creek, the children giggled. 'Coming ready or not!'

Then a terrifying holler came from the camp. 'Hush children. They're coming! Hide. HIDE!'

Maggie buried herself deep
into her mother's skirt.
No one stirred.

*The children scattered.
Hiding in the thick mud,
they lay silent. Still.*

THUD! Maggie slipped. Losing grip of her mother's hand, she found herself trapped in a sea of legs.

A truck rumbled along the bank like thunder.

Out stepped four heavy boots. THUD! THUD! THUD! THUD!

White men!

The children trembled.

Maggie crawled frantically to find her mother.
Hot tears ran down her cheeks.

The children were found. Screams echoed across the land as they scrambled to escape, sliding in the mud with every step.

A tender hand touched Maggie's shoulder.

'Mummy!' she gasped. 'I thought you were gone!'

The land wailed as the children were herded one by one onto the back of the truck.

Then it sped off, leaving behind only billowing dust.

Long ago and not so long ago, the children were taken away.

'We say sorry!' said the man.

Maggie's mother wiped her tears.

'To the mothers and the fathers, the brothers and the sisters ... we say sorry.'

Maggie listened. Her mother kissed her softly.

'SORRY.'

The word echoed around.

Every hand squeezed a little tighter.

'As Prime Minister of Australia,' he said, 'I am sorry.'

NATIONAL SORRY DAY

Not very long ago in Australia, it was government policy to remove Aboriginal and Torres Strait Islander children from their families. From 1910 to 1970, thousands of children were taken by government authorities. Today these children are known as the Stolen Generations.

White Australians living in the early 1900s believed that Aboriginal and Torres Strait Islander children were disadvantaged and at risk in their own communities. They thought that these children would receive a better education, a more loving family and a superior upbringing if they were adopted by white families or placed in government institutions.

In 1937, the Australian Government decided that all Aboriginal and Torres Strait Islander children who were not 'full blood' should be 'assimilated' into the wider white population. Children were taken from their families by force and were sent far away, all over Australia. Many of these children never saw their biological families again. Once removed, they were taught English and educated in Western ways. Some of the very young children did not even discover their Indigenous heritage until much later in life.

Families were torn apart and prevented from teaching their children about their Indigenous culture. Important connections to traditions, language, community and country were broken forever. Generations later, people are still feeling the trauma and grief.

On 10 December 1992, Prime Minister Paul Keating gave a historical speech in Redfern Park in Sydney to launch Australia's celebrations for the 1993 International Year of the World's Indigenous People. He was the first Australian political leader to publicly acknowledge the wrongs suffered by Aboriginal and Torres Strait Islanders in Australia.

13 February 2008—the day Prime Minister Kevin Rudd made the apology to the Stolen Generations on behalf of the Australian Government at Parliament House, Canberra.

The poster on the right was produced for the 1998 NAIDOC (National Aborigines and Islanders Day Observance Committee) week—a week of activities around Australia that celebrate Aboriginal and Torres Strait Islander histories, cultures and achievements.

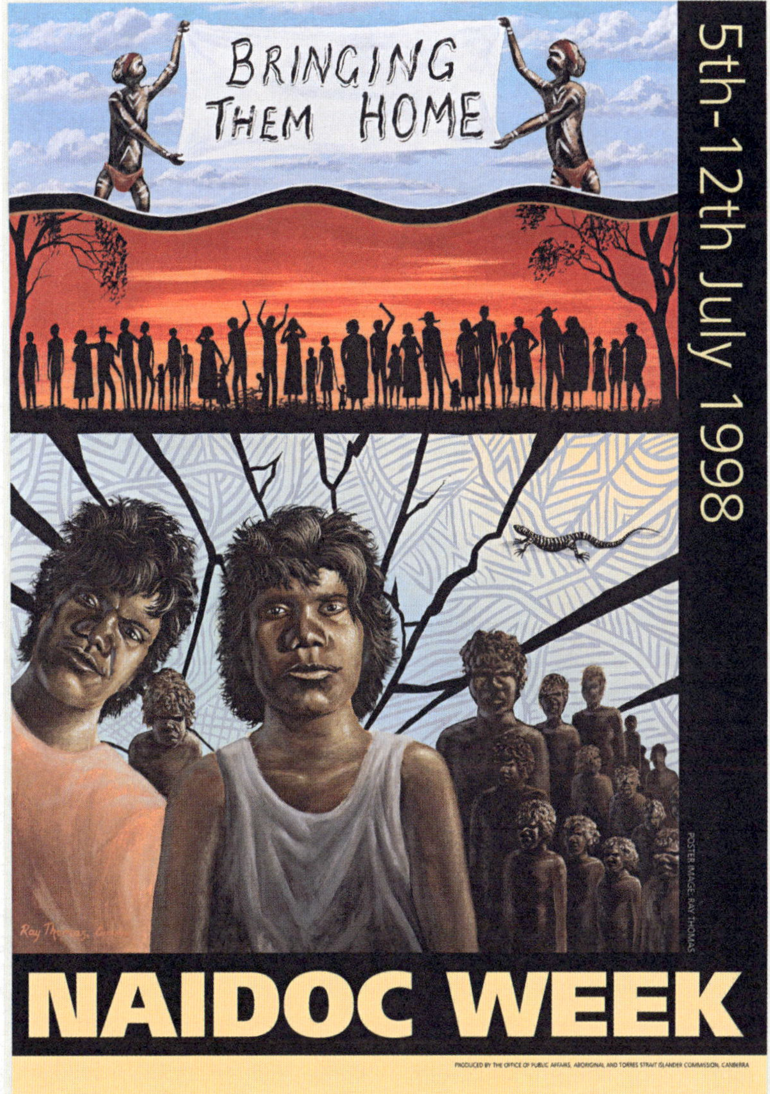

On 11 May 1995, the Attorney-General of Australia, Michael Lavarch, established an inquiry into the forced separation of Aboriginal and Torres Strait Islander children from their families. The inquiry was undertaken by the Human Rights and Equal Opportunity Commission and resulted in the report called *Bringing Them Home*. The presentation of the 680-page document to federal parliament on 26 May 1997 was a momentous event in Australia's history. The report helped to identify the needs of the victims and their families, and recommended provisions of services to those affected. A year later, on 26 May 1998, the first National Sorry Day was held.

However, it wasn't until 13 February 2008 that the Prime Minister, Kevin Rudd, on behalf of the Australian Government, made a public apology to the people of the Stolen Generations and their families. Every year since then, on 26 May, the anniversary of the apology is celebrated all over Australia as National Sorry Day.

If you are interested in finding out more about the Stolen Generations and National Sorry Day, explore the National Library of Australia's 'Bringing Them Home Oral History Project'. This is a collection of 340 recorded stories of Indigenous people and others, such as missionaries, police and administrators, involved in or affected by the process of child removals. These oral histories are of enormous historical significance and you can listen to many of them online, through the Library's catalogue (catalogue.nla.gov.au), where you can also find a wide range of other material on Australia's Indigenous histories and cultures.

Published by National Library of Australia Publishing
Canberra ACT 2600

ISBN: 9780642279651

The National Library of Australia acknowledges Australia's First Nations Peoples—the First Australians—as the Traditional Owners and Custodians of this land and gives respect to the Elders—past and present—and through them to all Australian Aboriginal and Torres Strait Islander people.

First Nations Peoples are advised this book contains depictions and names of deceased people, and content that may be considered culturally sensitive.

Editors: Irma Gold and Joanna Karmel
Designer: Amy Cullen
Printed in China through Asia Pacific Offset on FSC®-certified paper.

Access teachers' notes at coralvass.com/teachers-resources.

Find out more about NLA Publishing at library.gov.au/nla-publishing.

A catalogue record for this book is available from the National Library of Australia.

LIST OF ILLUSTRATIONS

Craig Mackenzie (b.1969)
An Aboriginal Australian Participating in a Smoking Ceremony to Mark the Apology to the Stolen Generations at Parliament House, Canberra, 13 February 2008
digital colour photograph
nla.gov.au/nla.cat-vn4545164

Damian McDonald (b.1971)
Aboriginal Flag Being Held up in Front of Parliament House for the Apology to the Stolen Generations of Australia, Canberra, 13 February 2008
digital colour photograph
nla.gov.au/nla.cat-vn4546550

Damian McDonald (b.1971)
Outside Parliament House during the Apology to the Stolen Generations, Canberra, 13 February 2008
digital colour photograph
nla.gov.au/nla.cat-vn4534549

Damian McDonald (b.1971)
Spectators Waving Flags while Watching a Big Screen Telecast of the Apology to the Stolen Generations at Parliament House, Canberra, 13 February 2008
digital colour photograph
nla.gov.au/nla.cat-vn4546273

June Orford (b.1946)
Prime Minister Kevin Rudd on the Big Screen in Federation Square during the Apology to the Stolen Generations, Melbourne, 13 February 2008
digital colour photograph
nla.gov.au/nla.cat-vn4502862

Ray Thomas (b.1960)
Bringing Them Home, NAIDOC Week 5th–12th July 1988
colour poster, 60 x 42cm
(Canberra: National Aborigines and Islanders Day Observance Committee, 1998)
nla.gov.au/nla.cat-vn6002191
© Ray Thomas/Copyright Agency, 2019

Aboriginal Flag © Harold Thomas